Away in a Manger
All artwork © 2005 Thomas Kinkade Studios, Morgan Hill, CA
A Parachute Press Book

Manufactured in China.
address HarperCollins Children's Books, a division of
HarperCollins Publishers, 10 East 53rd Street,
New York, NY 10022.
www.harpercollinschildrens.com

Library of Congress Cataloging-in-Publication Data is available.
ISBN 978-0-06-078730-1 (trade bdg.) — ISBN 978-0-06-078733-2 (lib. bdg.)
ISBN 978-0-06-078734-9 (pbk.)

Typography by Jeanne L. Hogle
09  10  11  12  13   SCP   10 9 8 7 6 5 4 3 2 1
❖
First Edition

# THOMAS✟KINKADE
# Away in a
# Manger

Thomas Kinkade Studios
**HARPER**
*An Imprint of HarperCollinsPublishers*
❀ A Parachute Press Book

"Away in a Manger" has always been one of my favorite Christmas carols because of its lovely simplicity. From toddler to adult, almost anyone at any age can understand the words and envision the images they create: a baby asleep, the stars shining down, lambs and sheep peacefully watching nearby. Such simple words—but what a story they tell.

Christmas has so much meaning for my family and me. It brings into play feelings of faith, of home, of tradition, and of hope. But it's good to remember that at its heart, Christmas is about the birth of our Lord. It's a story of light and joy—a light and joy that I wanted to capture for families like yours and mine.

I hope your family will share and enjoy this book, which conveys the miracle of the birth of the Baby Jesus and which ends with a prayer that all our children be protected and safe in his love and in ours.

God bless!

Thomas Kinkade

*Away in a manger, no crib for a bed,*

The little Lord Jesus laid down his sweet head.

The stars in the sky
looked down where he lay,
The little Lord Jesus
asleep in the hay.

The cattle are lowing, the baby awakes,
But little Lord Jesus, no crying he makes.

I love thee, Lord Jesus,
look down from the sky,

And stay by my cradle
till morning is nigh.

Be near me, Lord Jesus,
I ask thee to stay
close by me forever

And love me, I pray.

Bless all the dear children
in thy tender care,

And take us to heaven
to live with thee there.

The cattle are lowing, the baby awakes,

But little Lord Jesus, no crying he makes.

I love thee, Lord Jesus, look down from the sky,

And stay by my cradle till morning is nigh.


Be near me, Lord Jesus, I ask thee to stay

Close by me forever and love me, I pray.

Bless all the dear children in thy tender care,

And take us to heaven to live with thee there.